For my love, my life,
my Smooshy Face: Russell Farhang

&

Olympus
(the cat who didn't come inside for four years)


This book was made possible with help from my wonderful family.

My father, *Louis Carrozza*, altered the childhood dollhouse he built for me.

My mother, *Frances Carrozza*, sewed the curtains and assisted.

My sister, *Christina Carrozza D'Allesandro*, designed the clothing.

The rest of the Carrozza, Beaulieu, and O'Dell clans gave me inspiration and support.

I thank and love them with all of my heart.


Thank you to my editor, *Kate O'Sullivan*,

to my designer, *Brian Azer*,

to my photography guru, *Ted Sabarese*,

and to the Houghton Mifflin team,

especially *Sheila Smallwood* and *Pam Consolazio*

———◆———

www.houghtonmifflinbooks.com

Illustrations by Cynthia von Buhler
Book design by Brian J. Azer
The text of this book is set in P22 Mayflower and P22 Kilkenny.

Library of Congress Cataloging-in-Publication Data
Buhler, Cynthia von.
The cat who wouldn't come inside : Based on a true story / written and illustrated by Cynthia von Buhler.
p. cm.
Summary: In this cumulative story, a patient girl uses a growing number of enticements to gain the trust of a stray cat.
ISBN 0-618-56314-8 (hardcover)
1. Feral cats–Juvenile fiction. [1. Feral cats–Fiction. 2. Cats–Fiction.] I. Title: Cat who would not come inside. II. Title.
PZ10.3.B784 2006
[E]–dc22
2005033356
ISBN-13: 978-0-618-56314-2

Printed in China
SCP 10 9 8 7 6 5 4 3 2 1

# The Cat
# Who Wouldn't
# Come Inside

*Based on a True Story*

by *Cynthia von Buhler*

𝕺n a cold winter day, I looked out my window, and on my porch sat a cat with snow on his back. I opened the door and said, "Come inside, kitty!"

The cat ran away.

The next day, I left warm milk for the cat. When the cat came back, he lapped up all of the milk.

After the cat finished, I said, "Come inside, kitty!"

The cat ran away.

The next day, I left warm milk and a plate of tuna for the cat. When the cat came back, he lapped up all of the milk and ate the tuna. After he finished, I said, "Come inside, kitty!"

The cat ran away.

The next day, I left some warm milk, a plate of tuna, and a catnip mouse for the cat.

When the cat came back, he lapped up all of the milk, ate
the tuna, and pounced on the catnip mouse. After he finished,
I said, "Come inside, kitty!"

The cat ran away.

The next day, I left some warm milk, a plate of tuna, a
catnip mouse, and a soft rug for the cat.

When the cat came back, he lapped up all of the milk, ate
the tuna, pounced on the catnip mouse, and cleaned himself on
the soft rug. After the cat finished, I said, "Come inside, kitty!"

The cat ran away.

The next day, I left some warm milk, a plate of tuna, a
catnip mouse, a soft rug, and a ball of yarn for the cat.

When the cat came back, he lapped up all of the milk, ate the tuna, pounced on the catnip mouse, cleaned himself on the soft rug, and rolled around with the yarn. After the cat finished, I said, "Come inside, kitty!"

The cat ran away.

The next day, I left some warm milk, a plate of tuna, a catnip mouse, a soft rug, a ball of yarn, and a cozy armchair for the cat.

When the cat came back, he lapped up all of the milk, ate the tuna, pounced on the catnip mouse, cleaned himself

on the soft rug, rolled around with the yarn, and took a nap on the cozy armchair. After the cat finished, I said, "Come inside, kitty!"

The cat ran away.

The next day, I left some warm milk, a plate of tuna, a
catnip mouse, a soft rug, a ball of yarn, and a cozy armchair,
and I built a wall for the cat.

When the cat came back, he lapped up all of the milk, ate
the tuna, pounced on the catnip mouse, cleaned himself on

the soft rug, rolled around with the yarn, took a nap on the cozy armchair, and scratched the wall. After he finished, I said, "Come inside, kitty!"

The cat ran away.

The next day, I left some warm milk, a plate of tuna, a
catnip mouse, a soft rug, a ball of yarn, and a cozy armchair,
and I put wallpaper up and built a fireplace for the cat.
When the cat came back, he lapped up all of the milk, ate

the tuna, pounced on the catnip mouse, cleaned himself on the
soft rug, rolled around with the yarn, took a nap on the cozy
armchair, scratched the wall, and read a book by the fire. After
the cat finished, I said, "Come inside, kitty!"

The cat ran away.

The next day, I left some warm milk, a plate of tuna, a catnip mouse, a soft rug, a ball of yarn, and a cozy armchair, and I
put up curtains, built a fire, and left knitting needles for the cat.
When the cat came back, he lapped up all of the milk, ate
the tuna, pounced on the catnip mouse, cleaned himself on the

soft rug, rolled around with the yarn, took a nap on the cozy armchair, scratched the wall, read a book by the fire, and knitted a scarf.
After the cat finished, I said, "Come inside, kitty!"

The cat said, "No, *you* come inside."

And I did.

# Author's Note

This true story is about love and trust and how gaining trust takes time.

One winter day when I was living in Boston in a large purple Victorian house, a cat appeared on my porch. He was mangy and covered with snow. He was very afraid; I think he had been abused. He was also very fat. We called him Olympus after the large mountain in Greece.

I asked him to come inside every day, but he wouldn't budge from that porch. Over the course of four years I left him milk, fed him tuna, gave him rugs, blankets, and a comfy chair, and built him a small purple and green house, which was heated and had a bed for him.

Olympus's fur was tangled and dirty. Every day I tried to comb his matted coat, but he hissed and ran away. Finally, one afternoon he let me cut away the big snarl. He even let me pet him a little. After a while he'd whack at me to get petted because he liked it so much. I don't think that anybody had touched him gently before.

By the third year, Olympus started to let my friends pet him, too—even the postman knew and greeted him. But he still would not dare cross that threshold and come into my house. In the fourth year, almost overnight, Olympus became thin and weak. The vet said he was very sick. That same night, Olympus came inside. I held the door open and said, "Come inside, kitty" and finally he walked right in. He died in my arms that night. I was very sad, but at least Olympus had finally known great love in his life.

Olympus was afraid of people because he was a feral cat. Some people think that cats belong outside because their wild cat ancestors lived outside, but domestic cats are not well suited to the outdoors. Being out on the street can be unsafe for cats: they can get hit by cars and become injured by predators, and they often catch terrible diseases. They also breed with other cats and then their kittens become feral stray cats, too.

If you find a stray cat, call a reputable rescue service in your area. Make sure that the rescue service brings the cat to a no-kill shelter; otherwise the kitty might get put to sleep. Be sure to keep your own cat off the street, and make sure he wears a collar with a tag that clearly states your address and phone number in case he gets outside. (Use safe "pull-away" collars, because many collars can get caught on objects and choke your kitty.) If your cat must go outside, or if he constantly tries to get outside, consider having him microchipped in addition to wearing a safe collar with a tag. If he gets lost or injured and ends up at a shelter, he will be scanned and then you'll receive a call so you can have your cat returned to you.

# How the book was created:

The characters in this book were created using Sculpey™ clay. They were baked in an oven until hardened, cooled, and then decorated with gouache paint. The clothing was sewn by hand and frayed to look aged. The house was built by hand from wood and painted using latex outdoor house paints with a crackle glaze between the layers to age the surface. The snow was created from five different varieties of artificial snow, including spray snow and cotton batting. The icicles were made using a clear-gel glue. The set was photographed with a 2 x 4 Haselblad camera utilizing a variety of lenses and colored gel filters. The falling snow is the only element in the book that is an after-effect; it was created on a computer with Photoshop.

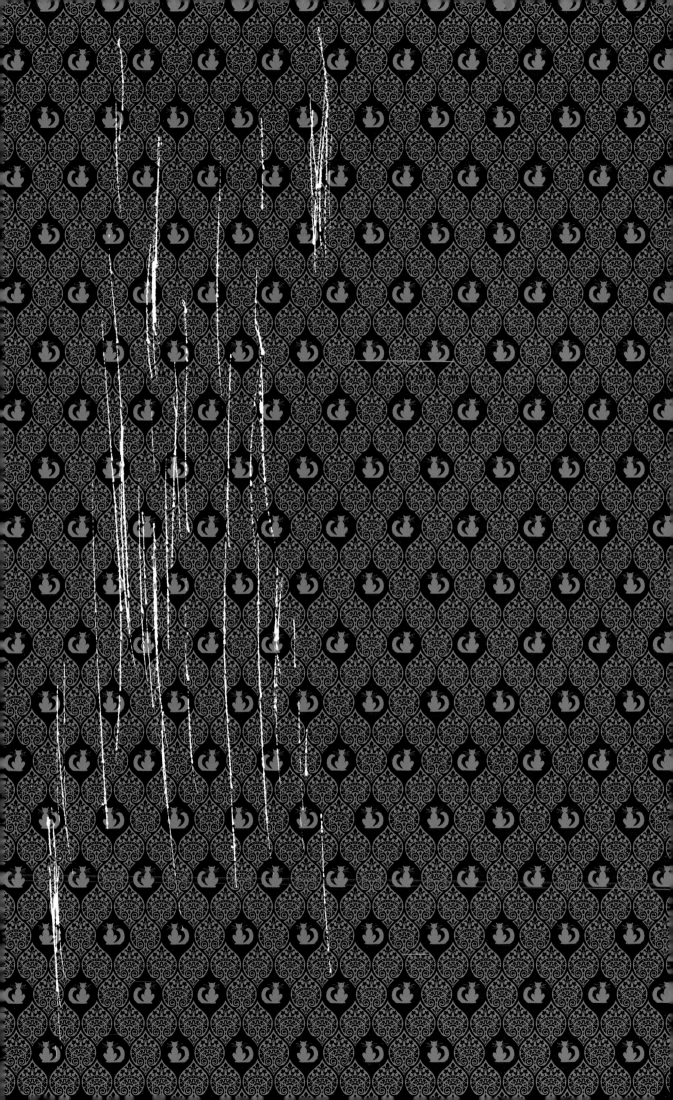